# The Gift in the Giant Blue Box

By

**Kerry Batchelder**

# A Grandma Batchie Book

**ISBN:** 9781688228856
**Imprint:** Independently published

Cover Design: https://www.fiverr.com/unique_graphic2
E-mail: uniquegraphic200@gmail.com

# Acknowledgements

To my husband, Scott,

    thank you for your ongoing encouragement and support in writing for children.


To my children, Sarah and Jeff,

    thank you for your continual support and encouragement as you have read and re-read my stories over the years.


To my mother, Susan,

    thank you for your valuable input in offering ideas and suggestions for the book.

# About the author

Kerry Batchelder has enjoyed writing stories for children for over forty years as a hobby.

She is now publishing her second book under the pen name, "Grandma Batchie," with "The Gift in the Giant Blue Box," being the second in its series.

Through her writing she hopes to capture the imagination of young children, while promoting laughter and good moral values.

Sitting alone on a cold,
frosty slope
among the
snow covered rocks,

I heard a soft voice
and looked down the
hill.
I saw his red hair and
bright socks.

He wore a fur hat
and carried a stick.
He smiled as he looked
at a fox.


Calling my name
he held something up,
a gift in a giant blue
box.

"Good friend," he said in a small quiet voice. "I want to give you this box."

"This gift is for you. I hope it's enough. It's full of new fancy socks."

Smiling, he shook
the entire box out.
He was up to his neck
in bright socks.

A rainbow of colors
in warm, fuzzy shades.
Some tied up in
cute little knots.

"What shall I do with
these socks, I
asked, with ten toes,
two feet in all?"

"Have a sock party
and give them as gifts
or throw the rolled
socks at a wall?

"Make a sock quilt
or a monkey from
socks?"
"Perhaps a cute
blanket or two?"

"Just take your old
socks back down the
hill and give them all
to the Zoo!

Sadly he turned
to go down the hill,
he gathered the
socks tenderly.

I felt a small tug on
my hand and looked
down.
A small Lox was
looking at me.

"I love the new socks,
so fuzzy and warm,
I'll take them all
up the hill."

"We all need new
socks, these are quite
nice and warm in the
cold winter chill."

So helping him
pack all those socks
up the hill,

I placed them in
each small Lox hand.

They welcomed me
in and gave me
Lox soup,
made fresh from the
crops of their land.

I met the Lox families,
youngest to old.
They could not offer
me much.

I realized how much
the socks meant to
them.
Through their kind
ways I was touched.

"More socks, I
shouted, and fuzzy,
warm gloves!"
"More food and clothes
I will bring."

"You've caused me to
see how selfish
I've been, I now
understand
everything."

Smiling, I left and ran down the hill to prepare more gifts for the Lox.

My life had so
changed.
I wanted to thank the
man with the
giant blue box.

Made in the USA
Columbia, SC
11 June 2022